WITHDRAWN
from the school library because
it is worn, damaged, out-of-date,
or no longer needed.

W9-BVL-908

But the prettiest card of all smells
of lavender and only says,
"From your Secret Valentine."

On Valentine's Day I get lots of letters!

Mommy says it's a day for people to tell me that they love me, too.

There is a card from Mommy, a card from Daddy, a card from Grandma, and even a card from Muffety.

Then I put my valentines into envelopes.

Mommy addresses them and we take them to the mailbox.

I draw a rainbow on a card for the old lady next door.

I write lots of kisses on Grandma's card, and I draw a fish on Muffety's card.

I draw lots of hugs on Daddy's card.

Then I draw pictures on the cards with my crayons. I draw a flower on Mommy's card.

Mommy helps me to cut out
paper hearts.
I glue the hearts and the
doilies onto my cards.

On the way home I see the old
lady who lives next door.
She looks lonely.

We see lots of valentine cards in the store.

But Mommy and I are going to make our own cards. We buy red paper and lacy doilies.

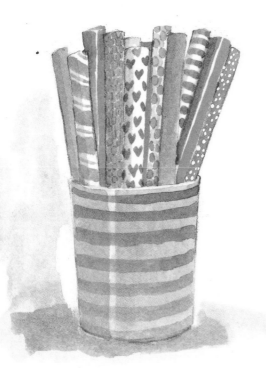

"I love lots of people," I say. "I love you and Daddy and Grandma and Muffety."

Muffety is my cat.

Valentine's Day is coming soon.
Mommy says it's a day to tell
people that you love them.

Secret Valentine

BY CATHERINE STOCK

BRADBURY PRESS · NEW YORK

COLLIER MACMILLAN CANADA
Toronto
MAXWELL MACMILLAN INTERNATIONAL PUBLISHING GROUP
New York   Oxford   Singapore   Sydney

VICTORY VILLA ELEMENTARY SCHOOL
LIBRARY
Compass and Honeycomb Roads
Baltimore, Maryland 21220

For Michael

Copyright © 1991 by Catherine Stock. All rights reserved.
No part of this book may be reproduced or transmitted in
any form or by any means, electronic or mechanical,
including photocopying, recording, or by any information
storage and retrieval system, without permission in
writing from the Publisher. Bradbury Press, Macmillan
Publishing Company, 866 Third Avenue, New York, NY
10022. Collier Macmillan Canada, Inc., 1200 Eglinton
Avenue East, Suite 200, Don Mills, Ontario M3C 3N1.
Printed in Hong Kong by South China Printing Company
(1988) Ltd. First American Edition   2   3   4   5   6
7   8   9   10   The text of this book is set in 20 point
Palatino. The illustrations are rendered in watercolor.
Book design by Catherine Stock.

Library of Congress Cataloging-in-Publication Data.
Stock, Catherine.   Secret valentine   /   by Catherine
Stock. — 1st ed.   p.   cm.   Summary: A child
makes valentines for her family and then adds a special
name to her list. On Valentine's Day she receives a secret
valentine in return.   ISBN 0-02-788372-8   [1. Valentine's
Day—Fiction.]   I. Title.   PZ7.S8635Se   1991
[E]—dc20   90-1916   CIP   AC

DATE DUE			